The Okefenokee Swamp

In southern Georgia, lapping just slightly over into northern Florida, is a 680-square-mile wilderness called the Okefenokee Swamp. Growing out of the dark swamp waters are dense forests of baldcypresses. These cypress forests are sometimes called the *swampy woods*. Land at the swamp's borders and islands within the swamp are covered with pine trees. These areas are sometimes called the *piney woods*. Where neither baldcypresses nor pines have taken hold, the waters of the Okefenokee form shallow marshes, waterways, and lakes. The *marshes*, also called *prairies*, are often completely covered with grasses and aquatic plants.

Spanish Moss

Spanish moss, a rootless plant that hangs on trees throughout the Okefenokee, is an *epiphyte* or air plant. It is able to get the nutrients it needs from air and rain.

Purple Gallinule

With its purple head and chest, green back, red and yellow bill, and bright yellow legs, the purple gallinule is perhaps the most colorful creature in the Okefenokee. This graceful water bird is usually seen walking on its long toes across water lily pads or wading in shallow water as it searches out its favorite foods — seeds, snails, insects, and frogs.

Baldcypress

The baldcypress is the king of the Okefenokee swampy woods. These trees can grow to be hundreds of years old, but because the largest old trees were cut down for their lumber early in this century, there are few, if any, ancient baldcypresses in the swamp. The baldcypress provides one of the most unusual features of the swamp — the knobby, cone-shaped cypress "knees" that grow up out of the water around the trees from underwater roots.

Alligator

Alligators are the largest reptiles in North America, and, although they can grow to twenty feet long, most are much smaller. There are about 12,000 'gators in Okefenokee Swamp. There used to be many more, but they were hunted and killed for their hides. The alligator is now a protected species, and its numbers are growing.

People in the Okefenokee

Seminole Indians made the Okefenokee their home until they were forced out in the 1830s. Later, homesteaders built small farms on islands within the swamp. At one time a businessman bought half the swamp from the state of Georgia and tried to drain it. He failed, but the twelve-mile-long canal he built remains. At the turn of the century, a lumber company built an elevated railroad to haul out the swamp's timber. A boom town grew up on one of the islands, populated by hundreds of lumbermen and their families. But within twenty years the valuable timber had been harvested, and the lumber company moved out. In 1937, Okefenokee Swamp became a National Wildlife Refuge. The trees have grown back, and almost every trace of civilization is gone.

Florida Cooters

Florida cooters can be seen basking in groups on partially submerged logs. If disturbed, the entire group will slide off the log in an instant. These turtles often lay their eggs in alligator nests.

Jackson's Plan

Written by **Linda Talley**

Illustrated by **Andra Chase**

MarshMedia, Kansas City, Missouri

To all friends of green things. L.T.

To Oscar and Ria. A.C.

Published by

A Division of Marsh Film Enterprises, Inc.
P. O. Box 8082
Shawnee Mission, KS 66208

Library of Congress Cataloging-in-Publication Data
Talley, Linda.
    Jackson's plan/written by Linda Talley; illustrated by Andra Chase.
        p.   cm.
    Summary: When he hears about a new tourist brochure to promote the Okefenokee Swamp in Georgia, Jackson the treefrog mounts a campaign to assure that treefrogs will be among the animals and plants featured.
    ISBN 1-55942-104-5
    [1. Tree Frogs—Fiction. 2. Swamp animals—Fiction.
3. Okefenokee Swamp (Ga. and Fla.)—Fiction.]
I. Chase, Andra, ill. II. Title.
PZ7.T156355Jac 1998
[Fic]—dc21   97-49606

Book layout and typography by Cirrus Design

Printed in Hong Kong

Special thanks to John Chase, Bud Dean, and Carol Talley.

It was afternoon at Okefenokee. In the green, swampy sunlight, Jackson dozed on a saw palmetto fan, dreaming of flies and mosquitoes and other delicious things.

Suddenly Jackson's eyes popped open. He heard a voice.

It was Judi, the park ranger.

"Well, Max," she was saying, "I'll meet you at the boat dock first thing in the morning. We'll get some great photos for our new brochure — pictures of all the things that bring folks to Okefenokee Swamp."

Jackson peered over the edge of his palm fan, his eyes bigger than ever. A long, froggy grin stretched across his face.

"Don't worry!" said Max, juggling his cameras. "We won't leave anything out. We'll have alligators and egrets, turtles and cranes, snakes and snipes, cypress trees and Spanish moss!"

Jackson's grin disappeared. "Humph!" he snorted. "What about treefrogs?"

"Are you speaking to me?" asked a voice.

A woodpecker stuck his head around a tree trunk.

"No, Fletcher," snapped Jackson. "I'm not!"

Jackson then told his friend Fletcher about the conversation he had overheard. Fletcher listened patiently. "Well, do you have a plan?" he asked.

Jackson was a bit startled by the question, but in the next instant, he knew with a certainty that there would be a green treefrog in the new Okefenokee Swamp brochure.

"Why, as a matter of fact, Fletcher, I do have a plan," Jackson said. "After all, it's simply a matter of sticking with it, isn't it? Wherever that photographer — that Max — goes, I'll be right there with him. When he goes to the swampy woods, I'll go to the swampy woods. When he goes to the marsh, I'll follow. When he goes to the piney woods, I'll be there too! I'll make sure there's a treefrog in that brochure!"

The next morning, Jackson hurried through the undergrowth, ready for his big day. But just as he hopped onto the boat dock, Judi dipped her paddle into the dark water and the canoe pulled away. Max had a camera to his eye and was already photographing the sights of Okefenokee.

But it was too early in the day for *this* treefrog to be discouraged. Defeat was not in Jackson's plan. He hurried as fast as he could to the end of the dock and leaped.

It wasn't good enough. The canoe glided away, leaving Jackson behind. Clinging to a neverwet, he watched the canoe grow smaller and smaller and then disappear into the swampy woods.

Jackson wasn't about to give up. He made his way to a knobby cypress knee growing out of the swamp waters. He climbed, then leaped to the next knee a few feet away — then to the next, the next, and the next. Birds squawked and flew out of his path.

Finally Jackson caught a glimpse of the canoe. Judi had stopped paddling so that Max could photograph an alligator.

Just seeing that alligator gave Jackson renewed
determination. On he leaped, from cypress to
holly to huckleberry.

He hopped over the alligator,
clambered onto a floating log and
across the turtles that were sunning
themselves there, then plopped
into the canoe.

"I think we got some really great photos here," Max was saying to Judi as she paddled on. "The alligator, the herons, the turtles — and that big old kingfisher."

"No treefrog?" puzzled Jackson

Suddenly they floated out of the gloom of the swampy woods into a vast sunfilled marsh.

Max hung over the edge of the canoe, photographing the water lilies and other plants that completely covered the surface of the water.

It occurred to Jackson that as long as he was in the canoe, he couldn't be in the picture. He made a great leap out onto a lily pad.

"Look at the beautiful orchids!" cried Max.

Jackson sprang into the middle of them.

"And look at the pipewort!" he exclaimed.

Jackson was there in an instant.

"And are those pitcher plants?" asked Max.

"Slow down!" gasped Jackson as he scrambled from one flower to the next. "I can't be in two places at once!"

"Now, Max," said Judi, "I have someplace else to take you." She dug her paddle into the water and swiftly pulled away, leaving Jackson hanging from a redroot stalk.

Jackson could see that on the far side of the marsh Judi had pulled the canoe ashore and that she and Max were trekking off into the piney woods. "I've got to get across this marsh, but how?" he sighed. The marsh looked so wide, much further than he could ever swim. But then, as if in answer to his question, a purple gallinule hurried by, stepping delicately from lily pad to lily pad with its large feet.

"Well, it's not an easy way, but it seems to be the only way across this marsh," said Jackson. "One lily pad at a time."

Judi and Max had not yet
returned to the canoe when
Jackson finally reached dry land.
"Just stick to your plan," Jackson
muttered to himself, and he
followed the trail into the piney
woods until he heard two voices.

"A photo of that woodpecker would
be fantastic," whispered Max. "If I could
just get a good angle on it."

Jackson looked up to see Fletcher, high in
a towering pine, higher than Jackson had ever
climbed. "Fletcher, it's me — Jackson," he called.
"Stay where you are! I'm coming up."

Up Jackson went. He looked down once and saw Max far below him, his camera to his eye. Jackson felt dizzy.

"Don't look down," Fletcher encouraged him.

Just as Jackson reached his friend, he heard Max cry out, "I got him! I got him! That's going to be a wonderful shot!"

Jackson happily made his way down the pine. All the way back to the canoe he was one step ahead of Max. He was beginning to understand what would catch his eye and so was always there . . . sharing a branch with the coachwhip snake . . . perched beside the cinnamon fern . . .

. . . on the shrub between Max's camera
and the white-tailed deer.

The sun was just setting as the canoe slid into the boat dock. Jackson was so tired he could barely jump out. But then he heard a familiar sound, something like the ringing of a cowbell from far away.

It was the song the green treefrogs sing at evening —
a perfect homecoming.

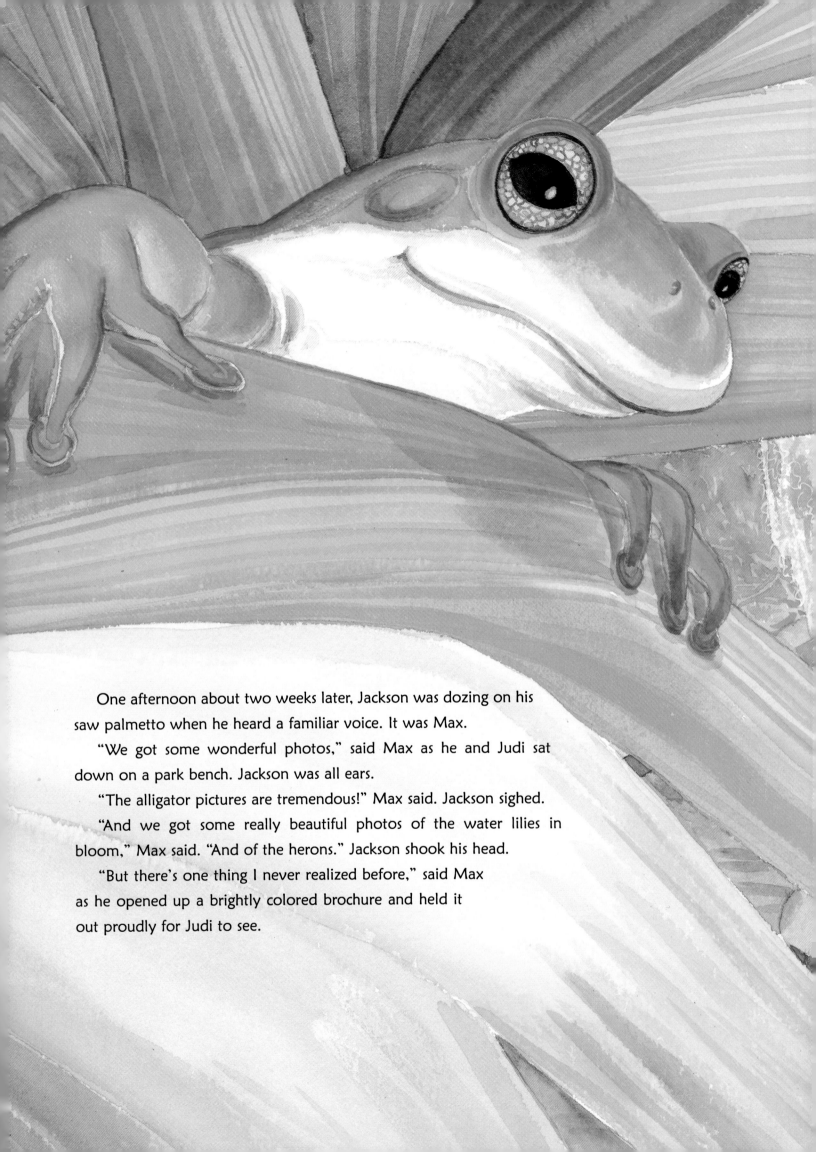

One afternoon about two weeks later, Jackson was dozing on his
saw palmetto when he heard a familiar voice. It was Max.

"We got some wonderful photos," said Max as he and Judi sat
down on a park bench. Jackson was all ears.

"The alligator pictures are tremendous!" Max said. Jackson sighed.

"And we got some really beautiful photos of the water lilies in
bloom," Max said. "And of the herons." Jackson shook his head.

"But there's one thing I never realized before," said Max
as he opened up a brightly colored brochure and held it
out proudly for Judi to see.

"I didn't know there were so many treefrogs in the Okefenokee!"

Pileated Woodpecker

Cinnamon

Water Lily

Coachwhip

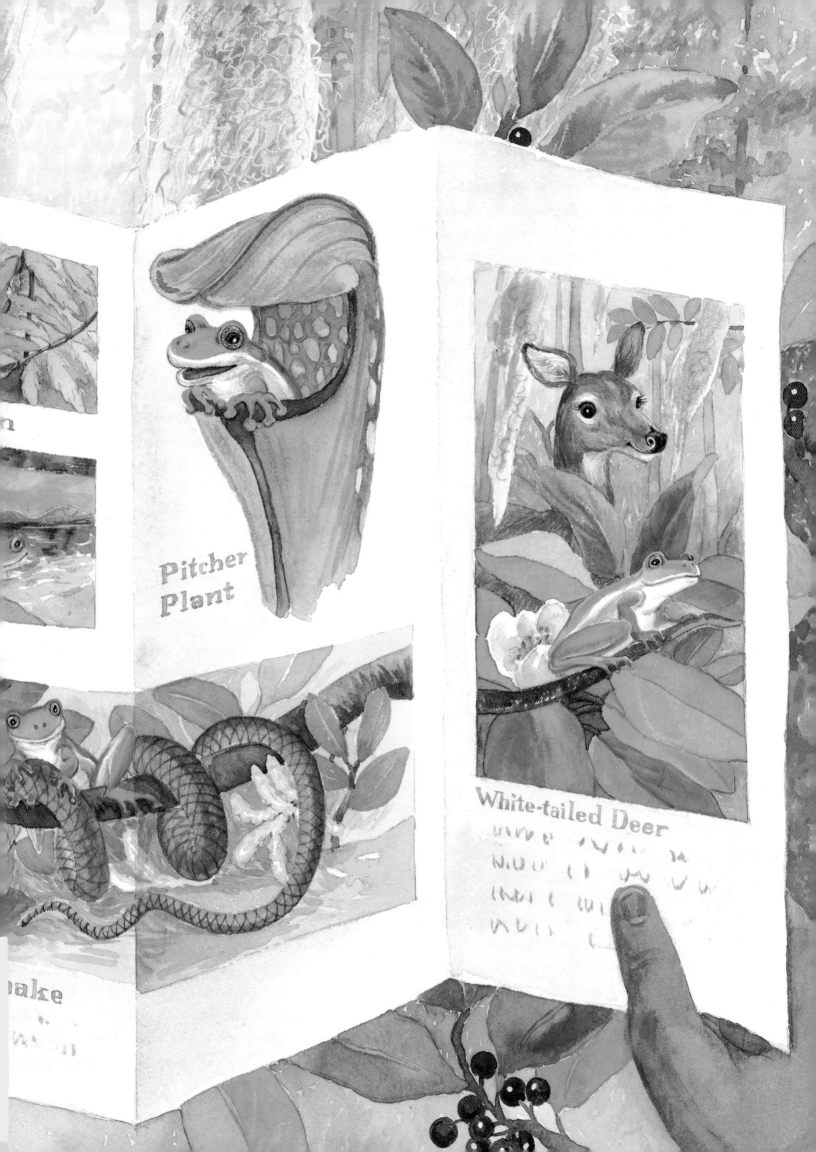

Pitcher
Plant

White-tailed Deer

...ake

It hadn't been easy, but Jackson had stuck to his plan, and he had succeeded.

He grinned a long froggy grin and returned to his dreams of dragonflies and beetles.

Dear Parents and Educators:

Perseverance is a habit that takes careful nurturing. It grows from enthusiasm for a cause, self-confidence, self-discipline, patience, and the willingness to practice. These skills work together to sustain us when success seems to be out of our reach.

As adults, we play an important role in helping children learn perseverance. We can begin by talking about our own goals and the plans we have in place to reach those goals, and we can analyze our mistakes and setbacks as learning experiences to demonstrate the positive attitude necessary to continue the journey.

We must also give children the opportunity to practice perseverance. Allowing children to experience their own low-risk struggles will help them learn to handle disappointment, frustration, confusion, and other emotions that accompany any endeavor. We must give young people the freedom to try, to sacrifice, and sometimes to fail in order for them to grow.

Encourage children to share their ideas and feelings about Jackson's experiences. Here are some questions to help initiate discussion about the message of *Jackson's Plan.*

- ✢ How did Jackson feel when he first heard the photographer talking about the brochure?

- ✢ What goal did Jackson set for himself?

- ✢ Did he have a plan to reach the goal?

- ✢ What were some of the things that went wrong?

- ✢ Did Jackson give up?

- ✢ How did Jackson feel at the end of the story?

- ✢ Was there ever a time when you kept trying even when it was hard work?

- ✢ How do you feel when you start something and then finish it?

Available from MarshMedia

Storybooks — Hardcover with dust jacket and full-color illustrations throughout.

Videos — The original story and illustrations combined with dramatic narration, music, and sound effects.

Activity Books — Softcover collections of games, puzzles, maps and project ideas designed for each title.

Amazing Mallika, written by Jami Parkison, illustrated by Itoko Maeno. 32 pages. ISBN 1-55942-087-1. Video. 15:05 run time. ISBN 1-55942-088-X.

Bailey's Birthday, written by Elizabeth Happy, illustrated by Andra Chase. 32 pages. ISBN 1-55942-059-6. Video. 18:00 run time. ISBN 1-55942-060-X.

Bea's Own Good, written by Linda Talley, illustrated by Andra Chase. 32 pages. ISBN 1-55942-092-8. Video. 15:00 run time. ISBN 1-55942-093-6.

Clarissa, written by Carol Talley, illustrated by Itoko Maeno. 32 pages. ISBN 1-55942-014-6. Video. 13:00 run time. ISBN 1-55942-023-5.

Gumbo Goes Downtown, written by Carol Talley, illustrated by Itoko Maeno. 32 pages. ISBN 1-55942-042-1. Video. 18:00 run time. ISBN 1-55942-043-X.

Hana's Year, written by Carol Talley, illustrated by Itoko Maeno. 32 pages. ISBN 1-55942-034-0. Video. 17:10 run time. ISBN 1-55942-035-9.

Inger's Promise, written by Jami Parkison, illustrated by Andra Chase. 32 pages. ISBN 1-55942-080-4. Video. 15:00 run time. ISBN 1-55942-081-2.

Jackson's Plan, written by Linda Talley, illustrated by Andra Chase. 32 pages. ISBN 1-55942-104-5. Video. 15:00 run time. ISBN 1-55942-105-3.

Jomo and Mata, written by Alyssa Chase, illustrated by Andra Chase. 32 pages. ISBN 1-55942-051-0. Video. 20:00 run time. ISBN 1-55942-052-9.

Kiki and the Cuckoo, written by Elizabeth Happy, illustrated by Andra Chase. 32 pages. ISBN 1-55942-038-3. Video. 14:30 run time. ISBN 1-55942-039-1.

Kylie's Concert, written by Patty Sheehan, illustrated by Itoko Maeno. 32 pages. ISBN 1-55942-046-4. Video. 17:20 run time. ISBN 1-55942-047-2.

Kylie's Song, written by Patty Sheehan, illustrated by Itoko Maeno. 32 pages. (Advocacy Press) ISBN 0-911655-19-0. Video. 12:00 run time. ISBN 1-55942-021-9.

Minou, written by Mindy Bingham, illustrated by Itoko Maeno. 64 pages. (Advocacy Press) ISBN 0-911655-36-0. Video. 18:30 run time. ISBN 1-55942-015-4.

Molly's Magic, written by Penelope Paine, illustrated by Itoko Maeno. 32 pages. ISBN 1-55942-068-5. Video. 16:00 run time. ISBN 1-55942-069-3.

My Way Sally, written by Mindy Bingham and Penelope Paine, illustrated by Itoko Maeno. 48 pages. (Advocacy Press) ISBN 0-911655-27-1. Video. 19:30 run time. ISBN 1-55942-017-0.

Papa Piccolo, written by Carol Talley, illustrated by Itoko Maeno. 32 pages. ISBN 1-55942-028-6. Video. 18:00 run time. ISBN 1-55942-029-4.

Pequeña the Burro, written by Jami Parkison, illustrated by Itoko Maeno. 32 pages. ISBN 1-55942-055-3. Video. 14:00 run time. ISBN 1-55942-056-1.

Plato's Journey, written by Linda Talley, illustrated by Itoko Maeno. 32 pages. ISBN 1-55942-100-2. Video. 15:00 run time. ISBN 1-55942-101-0.

Tessa on Her Own, written by Alyssa Chase, illustrated by Itoko Maeno. 32 pages. ISBN 1-55942-064-2. Video. 14:00 run time. ISBN 1-55942-065-0.

Time for Horatio, written by Penelope Paine, illustrated by Itoko Maeno. 48 pages. (Advocacy Press) ISBN 0-911655-33-6. Video. 19:00 run time. ISBN 1-55942-026-X.

Tonia the Tree, written by Sandy Stryker, illustrated by Itoko Maeno. 32 pages. (Advocacy Press) ISBN 0-911655-16-6. Video. 12:10 run time. ISBN 1-55942-019-7.

You can find storybooks at better bookstores. Or you may order storybooks, videos, and activity books direct by calling MarshMedia toll free at 1-800-821-3303.

MarshMedia has been publishing high-quality, award-winning learning materials for children since 1969. To receive a free catalog, call 1-800-821-3303.

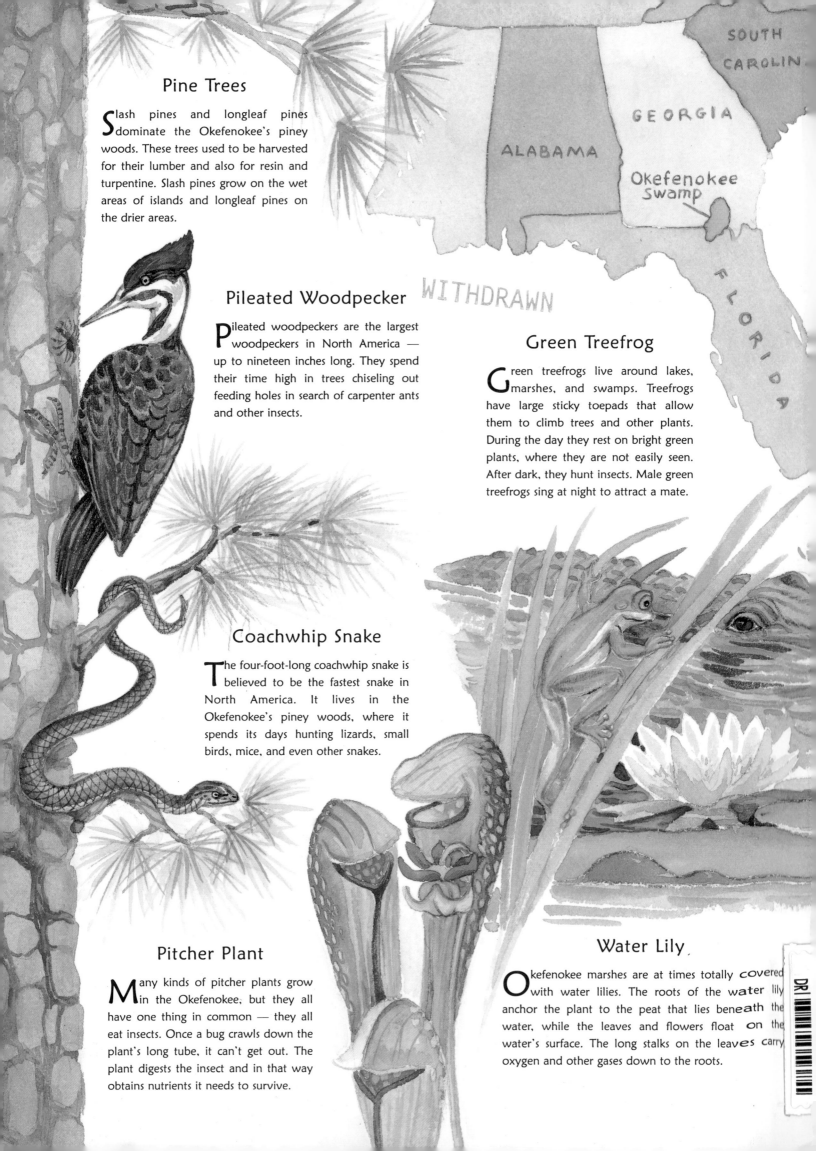

Pine Trees

Slash pines and longleaf pines dominate the Okefenokee's piney woods. These trees used to be harvested for their lumber and also for resin and turpentine. Slash pines grow on the wet areas of islands and longleaf pines on the drier areas.

ALABAMA

GEORGIA

SOUTH CAROLIN

Okefenokee Swamp

FLORIDA

Pileated Woodpecker

Pileated woodpeckers are the largest woodpeckers in North America — up to nineteen inches long. They spend their time high in trees chiseling out feeding holes in search of carpenter ants and other insects.

Green Treefrog

Green treefrogs live around lakes, marshes, and swamps. Treefrogs have large sticky toepads that allow them to climb trees and other plants. During the day they rest on bright green plants, where they are not easily seen. After dark, they hunt insects. Male green treefrogs sing at night to attract a mate.

Coachwhip Snake

The four-foot-long coachwhip snake is believed to be the fastest snake in North America. It lives in the Okefenokee's piney woods, where it spends its days hunting lizards, small birds, mice, and even other snakes.

Pitcher Plant

Many kinds of pitcher plants grow in the Okefenokee, but they all have one thing in common — they all eat insects. Once a bug crawls down the plant's long tube, it can't get out. The plant digests the insect and in that way obtains nutrients it needs to survive.

Water Lily

Okefenokee marshes are at times totally covered with water lilies. The roots of the water lily anchor the plant to the peat that lies beneath the water, while the leaves and flowers float on the water's surface. The long stalks on the leaves carry oxygen and other gases down to the roots.